THE LAUGH-A-MINUTE JOKE BOOK

Sonia Black & Pat Brigandi

illustrated by Don Orehek

SCHOLASTIC INC.
New York Toronto London Auckland Sydney

ISBN 0-590-42154-9

12 11 10 9 8   2 3 4/9

Printed in the U.S.A.   01

First Scholastic printing, May 1989

CONTENTS

ALL IN THE FAMILY

The nurse had just brought the baby twins to the window of the nursery. "What are their names?" asked an admirer.

"Steak and Kidney," answered the father.

"Don't mind my husband," said the mother quickly. "He's a little excited. He means Kate and Sidney."

Penny: Why is Daddy singing to the baby tonight?
Mother: He's trying to sing him to sleep.
Penny: If I were the baby, I'd pretend I was already asleep.

Sophia: Aunt Jane, have you heard that I'm engaged to an Irish boy?
Aunt Jane: Oh, really?
Sophia: No. O'Reilly.

Aunt Susie: That's a comet.

Eddie: A what?

Aunt Susie: A comet, Eddie. Don't you know what a comet is?

Eddie: No.

Aunt Susie: Don't you know what they call a star with a tail?

Eddie: Sure. Mickey Mouse.

Someone asked: Well, Johnny, what do you think of your new baby sister?

Johnny answered: If you want to know the truth, there are a lot of things we needed more around this house.

Mother: Why are you keeping this box of dirt, Willy?

Willy: That's instant mud-pie mix!

Susie: Mother, what was the name of the last station our train stopped at?

Mother: I don't know. Why?

Susie: Because that's where little Benny got off.

Peter: Mother, should you stir your tea with your left hand or your right hand?

Mother: Neither — use your spoon.

Father: Freddie, why is your face so red?

Freddie: I was running up the street to stop a fight.

Father: That's a very nice thing to do. Who was fighting?

Freddie: Me and Willie Smith.

Dad: Why are you scratching
   yourself, Wendy?
Wendy: Because nobody else
   knows where I itch.

The embarrassed city hostess said to her country cousin: "I thought I suggested you come after supper."

"Right," said the country cousin. "That *is* what I came after."

Jill: Stop reaching across the table. Haven't you got a tongue?
Jack: Yes, but my arms are longer!

Mrs. Smith: My daughter has arranged a little piece for the piano.
Next-Door Neighbor: Good! It's about time we had a little peace!

Son: Mom, I just knocked down the ladder that was standing against the side of the house.

Mom: Go and tell your father.

Son: He knows all about it. He's hanging onto the roof!

Father: Billy, this swing belongs to you and your brother. You must share it with him.

Billy: We always share it. I sit in the swing, and he pushes me.

Father: Why did you put a spider
in your sister's bed?
Son: Because I couldn't find a frog.

Mother: Eat your spinach. It'll put color in your cheeks.
Daughter: Who wants green cheeks?

Chloe: How did Mother find out that you didn't take a bath?
Joey: I forgot to wet the soap.

MONSTROUS GAGS

What's a vampire's favorite song?

"Fangs for the Memory."

First Witch: This special brew is making my legs smart.
Second Witch: Quick! Rub some on your head!

First Vampire: I've finally found the right ship for me, and I'm going to sea.
Second Vampire: What kind of ship are you going on?
First Vampire: A blood vessel.

Did you hear about the mummies
who went to the theater last night?

They gave the actors stage fright!

13

What did the father ghost say to his son?

Don't spook until you're spooken to.

What's a vampire's favorite animal?

A giraffe.

Why do Frankenstein monsters like jokes?

Because jokes keep them in stitches.

Which monster eats the fastest?

The goblin.

First Vampire: A beggar came up to me the other day and said, "I haven't had a bite in days."

Second Vampire: So what did you do?

First Vampire: What could I do? I bit him.

Monty Monster: That girl over there rolled her eyes at me. What should I do?

Milton Monster: If you are a real gentleman, you will pick them up and roll them back to her.

Ghoul Visitor: My, how your little ghoul has sprouted up! The last time I saw him, he was only so high.

Ghoul Mother: Yes, he certainly gruesome.

First Mummy: You know that big statue of a crouching lion with a human head that stands near the pyramids? Well, its nose is broken off.

Second Mummy: Really? Then how does it smell?

First Mummy: Smell! It sphinx!

If you ask your vampire if he wants something to eat, what might he say?

No fangs, I just ate necks-door.

First Woman: I hear you've fallen in love with Dracula.

Second Woman: Yes, it was love at first bite.

"There's a man here dressed in a black cape," said the nurse at the blood bank. "He has a strange request."

"What does he want?" asked the doctor.

"Well, sir," the nurse answered, "he's asking for two pints to go."

What happened to the Frankenstein monster who ate the electric company?

He went into shock.

Who is the mascot of the monster baseball team?

The bat boy.

What do witches eat on picnics?

Deviled eggs, deviled ham, and devil's food cake.

FOOD FOR THOUGHT

Why did the silly billy use a steam-roller on his farm?

He was trying to raise mashed potatoes!

How can you turn a pumpkin into a squash?

Throw it up in the air. It will come down — SQUASH!

Where were the first chickens fried?

In Greece!

Why did the cookie crumble?

Because its mother had been a wafer so long!

Johnny (offering some candy):
  Here, Janey, sweets to the sweet!
Janey: Oh, thank you, and won't
  you have some of these nuts?

Sign in a restaurant window:
  T-BONE STEAK, $1.00
Then, in fine print underneath:
  WITH MEAT, $12.00.

What did the hamburger say to the
ketchup bottle?

"That's enough out of you!"

Dolly: Do you know what Mary had when she went out to dinner?

Polly: Everybody knows Mary had a little lamb.

What is a cat's favorite breakfast?

Mice Krispies.

How do you make a cream puff?

Chase it around the block!

How do you keep peanut butter from sticking to the roof of your mouth?

Turn the bread upside down.

If 10 pickles are a bunch and 20 pickles are a barrel, how much are 30 and 40?

Seventy!

What's purple and wears a mask?

The Lone Grape.

Why did he become the Lone
Grape?

*He got tired of being one of the
bunch.*

What is the hamburgers' favorite
song?

"Home on the Range!"

Where do extra-smart frankfurters
end up?

On honor rolls.

Did you hear the joke about the sandwich?

Never mind. It's a lot of baloney.

Shopper: How much are your eggs?
Grocer: Eighty cents a dozen for the good eggs and fifty cents a dozen for the cracked eggs.
Shopper: Good. Crack me a dozen!

Customer: That chicken I bought yesterday had no wishbone.
Butcher: But it was a happy, contented chicken and had nothing to wish for.

Boy (in bakery): My mother says there was a fly in the raisin bread and she'd like to exchange it.

Baker: Tell your mother to bring me the fly, and I'll give her a raisin.

First Farmer: I see you're growing tomatoes. Tell me, why are some of them so poorly developed?

Second Farmer: Well, those are ketchup tomatoes. They start off slowly, but they ketchup by late spring.

Greedy Gracie sat down at the deli counter and ordered a whole pie.

"Shall I cut it into six pieces or eight?" asked the deli man.

"Six," said Gracie. "I'm on a diet."

French Chef: How do our French dishes compare with your American ones?

Tourist: They break just as easily.

Farmer's Son: Daddy, do you like baked apples?

Farmer: Yes, son. Why?

Farmer's Son: Because the orchard is burning!

Farmer Brown: Do you like raisin bread?

Farmer Smith: Can't say. Never raised any.

Dinner Guest: This beef stew tastes terrible.

Host: My wife has been making beef stew since before you were born!

Dinner Guest: Maybe so, but why did she save it for me?

ANIMAL CRACK-UPS

What do you get when you cross a porcupine with a gorilla?

An animal that always gets a seat on the bus.

What do you get when you cross an owl with a duck?

A real wisequacker.

What do you get when you cross a hyena with a chicken?

An animal that laughs at its own yolks.

What do you get when you cross an elephant with a kangaroo?

A *heavyweight boxer*.

What do you get when you cross a pig with a parrot?

An animal that hogs the conversation.

What do you get when you cross a boa constrictor with a lamb?

A wraparound sweater.

What do you get when you cross an electric eel with a goat?

An electric can opener.

What do you get when you cross a
duck with a rooster?

An animal that wakes you up at the
quack of dawn.

What do you get when you cross a
bull with a goose?

An animal that honks before it runs
you over.

What do you get when you cross a
cocker spaniel with a poodle and a
rooster?

A cockerpoodledoo.

What do you get when you cross
penguin with a leopard?

An animal in a polka-dot tuxedo.

What do you get when you cross an owl with an oyster?

An animal who's always dropping pearls of wisdom.

What do you get when you cross a shark with a parrot?

An animal that can talk your ear off.

What do you get when you cross an elephant with a lamb?

An animal that carries a sweater in its trunk.

What do you get when you cross a hyena with a collie?

An animal that laughs through Lassie movies.

What do you get when you cross a mink with a kangaroo?

A fur coat with a pocket in it.

What do you get when you cross a mole with a police dog?

An animal that will bring law and order to the underground.

What do you get when you cross an elk with a giraffe?

A hat rack for extremely tall people.

What do you get when you cross a parrot with a woodpecker?

An animal that talks in Morse Code.

What do you get when you cross a clam with a rooster?

A very quiet alarm clock.

CLASSROOM CHUCKLES

Sam had just completed his first day at school.

"What did you learn today?" asked his mother.

"Not enough," said Sam. "I have to go back tomorrow."

Suzie: Mother, I can't go to school today.
Mother: Why not?
Suzie: I don't feel well.
Mother: Where don't you feel well?
Suzie: In school.

Teacher: Milton, can you tell me how fast light travels?
Milton: I don't know, but it always gets here too early in the morning.

Horace: Day after day the boy and his dog went to school together until at last the day came when they had to part.

Morris: What happened?

Horace: The dog graduated.

Grandma: And how do you like going to school, Billy?

Billy: I like going, and I like coming back. It's the part in between I don't like.

Mother: I'm worried about your always being at the bottom of your class.

Sadie: Don't worry, Mom. They teach the same thing at both ends.

Teacher: Joe, give me the definition of a vacuum.

Joe (after thinking for a while, and pointing to his head): Gee whiz, I've got it up here, but I just can't explain it.

Laugh and the class laughs with you, but you stay after school alone.

Father: What's the meaning of those Ds and Fs on your report card?
Son: Oh, Dad, that mean's I'm Doing Fine.

Did you hear the one about the teacher who graded tests so carefully that she flunked two students for making their periods upside down?

Why do soccer players get good grades in school?

They use their heads.

Teacher: Name four seasons.
Student: Salt, pepper, sugar, and
   spice.

A politician was invited to give a
speech at a school. He talked and
talked for a long time, pausing only
to look at his watch. He then said
to the audience, "My watch has
stopped. Does anyone have a
watch?"

"No," said someone in the audience. "But there's a calendar behind
you!"

Teacher: Billy, how do you spell
   Mississippi?
Billy: Do you want the river or the
   state?

Teacher: When is the best time to pick the fruit from the trees?
Sally: When the farmer is asleep.

Teacher: Where were you born, William?
William: Texas.
Teacher: What part?
William: All of me.

Teacher: Tommy, what expression do students who don't study use most of all?
Tommy: I don't know.
Teacher: That's right!

Ted: I'm no longer the quarterback on our school's football team.

Ed: What happened?

Ted: It's all my mother's fault. She made me promise not to pass anything until somebody said, "Please!"

Teacher: Tom, name two pronouns.

Tom: Who, me?

Teacher: That's correct.

An absentminded professor came home late one night. When he reached his door, he realized he had forgotten his key. He knocked and knocked until finally his wife peeked out the door. Since it was very dark, she didn't recognize him.

"I'm sorry, sir," she said, "but the professor isn't home."

The professor, absentminded as usual, replied, "Okay, I'll come back tomorrow."

Student to teacher: Yesterday
you said five and five made ten, and
today you tell me that seven and
three make ten. Which one am I
supposed to believe?

Football Coach: Sidney, you can be the end, guard, and tackle.

Sidney: That's great, Coach! Thanks!

Football Coach: Yes, sit at the end of the bench, guard the water bucket, and tackle anyone who gets near it.

Teacher: Name one animal that lives in Africa.

Student: An elephant.

Teacher: Good. Next! You name another.

Second Student: Another elephant!

THE DOCTOR'S IN

Patient: Doctor, can I sleep in my
contact lenses?
Doctor: No, your feet would stick
out!

Patient: Doctor, do you think blue-
berries are healthy?
Doctor: Well, I've never heard one
complain.

Doctor: What is that tightwad
patient complaining about now?
Nurse: He says he got well before
all the medicine was used up.

A doctor and a bus driver were in
love with the same woman. The bus
driver had to go away for a week,
so he gave the woman seven apples.
Why?

*Because an apple a day keeps the
doctor away.*

The psychiatrist was testing his patient. "Do you ever hear voices without being able to tell who is speaking or where the voices are coming from?" he asked.

"Yes, sir," the patient replied.

"And when does this occur?" questioned the doctor.

"When I answer the telephone."

Doctor: How did you get here so fast?

Patient: Flu.

Did you hear the joke about the new surgeon doll?

You wind it up, and it operates on batteries.

Patient: My stomach's been aching ever since I ate those twelve oysters yesterday.

Doctor: Were they fresh?

Patient: I don't know.

Doctor: Well, how did they look when you opened the shells?

Patient: You're supposed to open the shells?

Prison Officer: Sir, I have to report that ten prisoners have broken out.

Warden: Blow the whistles, sound the alarms, alert the police —

Prison Officer: Shouldn't we call the doctor first? It looks as if it might be measles.

How long should doctors practice medicine?

Until they get it right.

What's round, white, and lifts weights?

An extra-strength aspirin.

What's the difference between a rug and a bottle of medicine?

One you take up and shake; the other you shake up and take.

Doctor: The check you gave me last week came back.
Patient: So did the pain in my chest.

Clara: Imagine meeting you here at the psychiatrist's office. Are you coming or going?
Maria: If I knew that, I wouldn't be here!

Bill: My doctor says I can't play
tennis.
Phil: Ah, he's played with you, too?

What did the doctor say to the
Invisible Man's wife?

*I can't see anything wrong with your
husband.*

What did the arthritis say to the
rheumatism?

Let's get out of this joint.

What did the appendix say to the kidney?

The doctor's taking me out tonight.

What makes a doctor angry?

Running out of patients.

Patient: Doctor, Doctor, people keep making fun of me.
Doctor: Get out of here, you silly fool!

Patient: Doctor, I keep thinking I'm a horse.

Doctor: Well, I can cure you, but it's going to cost you a lot of money.

Patient: Money's no problem. I just won the Kentucky Derby.

Cary: I know someone who thinks he's an owl.

Mary: Who?

Cary: Make that two people.

Mel: I've been seeing spots before my eyes lately.

Nell: Have you seen a doctor?

Mel: No, just spots.

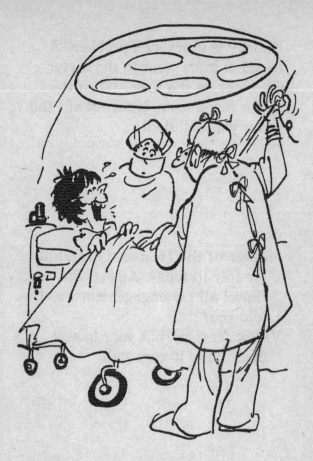

Wanda: I was operated on last week and really enjoyed it.

Wendy: How come?

Wanda: The doctor had me in stitches.

Ecology is everyone's problem. A friend of mine went to the doctor for water on the knee. When the doctor made tests, it turned out the water was polluted!

Master of the House: I'm feeling terribly ill today, Albert. Did you cancel all my engagements, as I told you?
Valet: Yes, sir, but your fiancé didn't take it very well.

Patient: Will my measles be better next week, Doctor?
Doctor: I don't like to make rash promises.

Patient: I'm worried. I keep thinking I'm a pair of curtains.
Psychiatrist: Stop worrying and pull yourself together.

Receptionist: Doctor Chaunchadinjhi is waiting for you, sir.
Patient: Which doctor?
Receptionist: Oh, no, he's fully qualified.

FORECAST FUNNIES

When can fifty people stand under an umbrella without getting wet?

When it's not raining!

Does the weather change quickly in the spring?

No, it only changes by degrees!

What is the best thing to keep in hot weather?

Cool!

Why did the lady go outside with
her purse open?

*She expected some change in the
weather!*

What did Frosty say when the weather reporter predicted a heavy snowfall?

"Snow news is good news!"

Polly: What's the weather like?
Molly: I don't know — it's so cloudy I can't see!

Did you hear about the nerd who cut a hole in his umbrella?

He wanted to know when it stopped raining!

What moves faster — hot or cold?

Hot. Everybody can catch cold!

Teacher: Jimmy, how do you spell
   rain?
Jimmy: R–A–N–E.
Teacher: That's the worst spell of
   rain we've had around here in a
   long time!

Iggy: Where do all the bugs go in
   the winter?
Ziggy: Search me.
Iggy: No, thanks. I just wanted to
   know.

Why did the man throw the ther-
mometer out the window?

*He wanted to watch the temperature
drop!*

Kitty: You remind me of London.

Catty: Because of my English accent?

Kitty: No, because you're always in a fog!

Why does it snow in the winter?

Because snow would melt in the summer.

What do you get if you cross a hurricane with a comedian?

Gales of laughter.

How is a winter day different from an unconscious boxer?

One is cold out, the other is out cold.

What happens after a dry spell?

It rains.

Customer: I want a winter coat.
Salesperson: How long?
Customer: For the whole winter, silly!

What are the best letters to read in hot weather?

Fan mail!

When do boxers start wearing gloves?

When the weather gets cold!

JUMBO LAUGHS

Ann: What do you find between elephants' toes?
Stan: Slow-running people.

Mike: Why are elephants such bad dancers?
Ike: Because they have two left feet.

Matt: What's the best way to raise an elephant?
Pat: Use a crane.

He: Why can't two elephants go into a swimming pool at the same time?

She: Because they have only one pair of trunks.

Tom: What do you do with a blue
elephant?
Dick: Cheer him up.

Terry: Why does an elephant have
a trunk?
Kerry: I don't know.
Terry : He would look pretty silly
with a glove compartment.

Bob: How do you get an elephant
into a matchbox?
Carol: Take out the matches first.

Paul: How do you make an elephant float?

Saul: Put two scoops of ice cream, some milk, and soda water in a glass. Add one elephant.

Ted: Where do you find elephants?

Ned: It depends on where you leave them.

Billy: What do you give a seasick elephant?

Tilly: Lots of room!

Hal: Why do elephants hide behind trees?

Sal: So they can trip ants.

Jill: How do you get down from an elephant?

Bill: You don't. You get down from a duck!

Tom: What is the best thing to do if you find an elephant in your bed?

Jerry: Sleep somewhere else.

Ed: How do you keep an elephant from going through the eye of a needle?

Edna: Tie a knot in its tail.

Moe: Why do elephants lie down?
Larry: They can't lie up.

Ted: What brings baby elephants?
Alice: Big storks.

Frank: How do you fit six elephants into your car?
Fran: Sit three in the front and three in the back.

Mark: Why do elephants have flat feet?

Clark: From jumping out of trees.

What kind of elephants live at the North Pole?

Cold ones!

SERVICE WITH A SMILE

Customer: Waiter, this salad tastes awful. Are you sure the lettuce was washed?

Waiter: Yes, sir. In fact you can still see the soap on it!

Customer: Waiter, why does this doughnut look all crushed?

Waiter: Well, you said coffee and a doughnut and step on it.

Customer: Waiter, there's a fly in my soup.

Waiter: Don't worry, sir. The spider on the bread will probably eat him.

Customer: Waiter, your thumb is touching my steak. Please remove it.

Waiter: What, and drop it again?

Customer: Waiter, this fish isn't as good as the fish I had last week.

Waiter: That's strange, sir. It's the same fish.

Waiter: How did you find the meat, madam?

Customer: I just looked under a potato chip, and there it was.

Customer: Waiter, this coffee tastes like tea.

Waiter: I'm sorry, madam; I must have given you the hot chocolate by mistake.

Customer: What's this fly doing in my soup?

Waiter: The backstroke, sir.

Customer: Waiter, is there soup on the menu?

Waiter: No, madam, I wiped it off.

Customer: Waiter, how old is this meat?

Waiter: I don't know, sir. I've only been here a year.

Customer: This goulash is terrible!
Cook: That's funny. I put a brand new pair of goulashes in it.

Customer: Have you any wild duck?

Waiter: No, sir, but we could take a tame one and irritate it!

Customer: Waiter, how did this fly get in my soup?

Waiter: I guess it flew in, sir.

Customer: Waiter, there's a twig in my soup.

Waiter: I wouldn't be surprised, sir. This restaurant has branches all over the city.

Customer: I can't eat this food. Call the manager.

Waiter: It's no use. He can't eat it, either.

Waiter: Have you tried the meatballs, sir?

Customer: Yes, and I found them guilty.

Customer: Waiter, there's a button in my salad.

Waiter: Oh, it must have come off when the salad was dressing.

Customer: Why is this chop so tough?

Waiter: Well, sir, it's a karate chop.

Customer: Waiter, there's a fly in my soup.

Waiter: Hold on, sir. I'll get you a fork.

KNOCK IT OFF!

Knock, knock.
Who's there?
Major.
Major who?
Major answer, didn't I?

Knock, knock.

Who's there?

Agatha.

Agatha who?

Agatha flu, so stay away from me.

Knock, knock.
Who's there?
Amos.
Amos who?
A mosquito bit me.

Knock, knock.
Who's there?
Andy.
Andy who?
Andy bit me again.

Knock, knock.
Who's there?
Alfred.
Alfred who?
Alfred the needle if you'll sew the
button on.

Knock, knock.
Who's there?
Tarzan.
Tarzan who?
Tarzan stripes forever.

Knock, knock.
Who's there?
Accordian.
Accordian who?
Accordian to the paper it's going to
 rain tonight.

Knock, knock.
Who's there?
Jamaica.
Jamaica who?
Jamaica passing grade in math?

Knock, knock. Who's there?

Heywood, Hugh, and Harry. Heywood, Hugh, and Harry who?

Heywood Hugh Harry up
and open this door?

Knock, knock.
Who's there?
Danielle.
Danielle who?
Danielle so loud; I can hear you.

Knock, knock.
Who's there?
Fanny.
Fanny who?
Fanny body calls, I'm out.

Knock, knock.
Who's there?
Ivan.
Ivan who?
Ivan waiting hours for you to answer the door.

Knock, knock.
Who's there?
Yvonne.
Yvonne who?
Yvonne to be alone.

Knock, knock.   Who's there?

Howard.   Howard who?

Howard is the ground when
you slip on a banana peel?

Knock, knock.
Who's there?
Shelby.
Shelby who?
Shelby coming 'round the mountain
    when she comes.

Knock, knock.
Who's there?
Police.
Police who?
Police open the door. Thank you.

Knock, knock.
Who's there?
Howell.
Howell who?
Howell I get in if you don't open the
   door?

Knock, knock.   Who's there?

Justin.   Justin who?

Justin time for dinner.

Knock, knock.
Who's there?
Murray Lee.
Murray Lee who?
Murray Lee we roll along. . . .

Knock, knock.
Who's there?
Orange.
Orange who?
Orange you glad this is over?